THE CORN CLOUD PROBLEM

by Anne O'Brien
illustrated by Scott Ross

Scott Foresman

Editorial Offices: Glenview, Illinois • New York, New York
Sales Offices: Reading, Massachusetts • Duluth, Georgia
Glenview, Illinois • Carrollton, Texas • Menlo Park, California

A family had a farm. They grew
corn on the farm. One day the
dad saw some clouds. And he had
an idea.

"Let's puff up the corn," he said.
"We can sell it as cereal. We can
call it Corn Clouds.

"New! Light! Corn Clouds!" the
box will say. "Out of this world!
Children love it!"

Corn Clouds were a big hit.
But the farm began to get calls.
When children ate Corn Clouds,
they got very light. They got so
light that they floated!

"We can not get our children down," parents said.

The farm family called a meeting. They would have to fix the problem.

"Should we stop selling Corn Clouds?" one son asked.

"But they are so good," said another.

"We must fix Corn Clouds,"
said the mom. "What can we add
that is heavy?"

"Raisins!" the little girl said.

From then on, Corn Clouds
made children light. But not too
light! The children were happy.
The parents were happy. And the
family on the farm was happy.